Soprano Trouble

Choir Girls, Book 1

Victoria Kimble

TouchPoint
Press

SOPRANO TROUBLE (Choir Girls Series, Book 1) by
Victoria Kimble
Published by TouchPoint Press
4737 Wildwood Lane
Jonesboro, AR 72401
www.touchpointpress.com

ISBN-10: 1542618894
ISBN-13: 978-1-54261-889-2

Editor: Melody Miller
Cover Design: Shayne Leighton

Visit the author's website at www.victoriakimble.com

First Edition

Printed in the United States of America.

Dedication

For my girls, Alaina, Joya and Bria. I pray that you will have the courage to influence others for the Lord, and that you will not be easily influenced by the world.

CONTENTS

Dedication	iii
Acknowledgments	i
Chapter 1	3
Chapter 2	12
Chapter 3	20
Chapter 4	28
Chapter 5	35
Chapter 6	41
Chapter 7	48
Chapter 8	55
Chapter 9	63
Chapter 10	69
Chapter 11	76
Chapter 12	83
Chapter 13	90
Chapter 14	97
Chapter 15	105
Chapter 16	112
Chapter 17	120
Coming Soon	124
About the Author	125

Acknowledgments

I'd like to thank my launch team and my Real Talk girls for being so excited about this story. Your encouragement has meant the world to me.

Chapter 1

"Hey, Summer, quit daydreaming! This is our stop."

Twelve-year-old Summer McKidd turned with a start from the bus window at the sound of Cammie Dunn's voice. She felt her face get hot as she gathered her black sparkle tote and red zip-up hoodie and hurried off the bus to join her friends. Cammie, Brittany Welsh, and Maddie Ryland stood on the sidewalk in the warm afternoon sun, watching Summer rush down the steps.

"You know, the view out the window isn't *that* interesting, Summer," Cammie said, her hands on her hips. "So what *were* you thinking about?"

"Maybe she was thinking about Mrs. Dean's math class," Brittany piped in, pushing her square glasses up on her button nose. "Or maybe she was thinking of who she sits by in

Mrs. Dean's math class." The two girls started giggling.

"No, no, the leaves are starting to change and I thought—" Summer choked. Her blush deepened as she tucked her shoulder-length curly brown hair behind her ears.

"Oh, stop," Maddie jumped in. "Let's not stand here all day." Maddie looped her arm through Summer's and tugged her up the street. "If you insist on talking about school, let's talk about choir." All four girls were in the 7th grade Concert Choir at Aspen Junior High. Their fall concert was in just two weeks, and one girl and one guy would get to sing a solo. It was a well-known fact that whoever got to sing the solo at the fall concert would also be featured in the Christmas concert.

"Oh my gosh, your audition was a-maz-ing, Cammie," Brittany gushed, her short, round frame bouncing in excitement. "I know Mr. Camp will pick you for the solo." Cammie smirked and tousled her short, spiky hair, her red highlights glittering in the sun.

"It was good, wasn't it?" Cammie replied. "I think it's smart to make us audition in front of the whole choir. It really lets Mr. Camp know who can handle that kind of pressure."

"Well, clearly I can't," Maddie stated, staring straight ahead. "My voice doesn't crack like that when I sing with the group. At least, it seemed like it was fine when we were learning the solo as a group."

"Maddie, you did just fine," Summer replied, patting Maddie on the arm. Summer hated to see her friend embarrassed.

"Don't worry about it," Maddie said, smiling at Summer. "I'm not scarred. I am actually perfectly content to get lost in the masses. I like to sing, and in the group the focus isn't directly on me. It's really the best of both worlds."

"Your only real competition is Pilar Sanchez," Brittany said, wrinkling her nose as she stressed the pronunciation of PEE-lar. "But I know you did better than her."

"Ugh, she is such a teacher's pet," Cammie grumbled. "Unfortunately, she's an excellent soprano. Maybe I should hang out in Mr. Camp's room all day too. Give her a run for her money."

"I think she's just shy," Summer said, trying to keep the conversation positive. "She probably feels more comfortable in there, since she doesn't seem to have many friends."

"Whatever," Cammie blurted, kicking at a pile of dead leaves. "She should know by now that no one will be friends with a teacher's pet. Hanging on Mr. Camp's every word is not going to get her anywhere."

"Yeah," Brittany echoed. "She can't be that serious about making friends."

"I really like the songs Mr. Camp picked out for the concert," Summer said, trying to change the subject.

"Me too. I wonder how many will showcase dear PEE-lar," Cammie replied. Brittany burst out laughing.

"This is our turn off," Maddie interrupted. "See you girls tomorrow." Maddie and Summer rounded the corner toward their houses as Cammie and Brittany laughed and turned in the other direction.

Summer had been friends with Cammie and Brittany since the third grade. The three of them had had countless sleepovers, dance parties, and giggle fests in their years as friends. Both Cammie and Brittany could be sarcastic and relentless in their teasing sometimes, but they were fun to be around and enjoyed singing as much as Summer did. She was happy to have them as friends, especially in seventh grade when everyone knows it's hard enough to make friends.

They had met Maddie this year in choir. She had moved to their town of Pinewood, Colorado just before school started. Maddie was also in math and language arts with the other three, and her locker was right next to Summer's. She seemed to be a perfect fit for their group.

"Are you really okay about your audition?" Summer asked Maddie, giving her a sideways glance as they walked. "I know Cammie is pretty proud of her voice, but your voice is really nice, too."

"Of course!" Maddie replied, gathering her long, dark blonde hair into a messy ponytail. "I do like to sing, but not as much as I like volleyball. I'd be devastated if I got second string in volleyball. Not getting the solo is no skin off my nose."

"Good," Summer said, satisfied that her friend was telling the truth and not hiding some inner pain. "I wonder if Cammie will get it. Pilar really was as good as her."

"I know. I have a feeling we'll never hear the end of it either way," Maddie said wryly. "Well, we'll find out tomorrow. See you then!" Maddie trotted up the walk to her house. She turned and waved at Summer before letting herself inside.

Three houses later, Summer was home. She walked past the potted chrysanthemums and in the front door, calling hello to her mom. Her 10-year-old sister, Faye, sat on the couch watching *Girl Meets World*.

"Hi, Summer!" she called, jumping up from her seat. "Do you want to watch *Girl Meets World* with me? Riley is wearing this really cute top I think you'll like."

"No, Faye," Summer replied with a scowl. "In seventh grade, we have actual homework." Faye quickly lost her smile, slumped down on the couch, and turned up the volume.

"Hi, Summer," Summer's mom said as she walked into the kitchen. "Need a snack?"

"No thanks. Just some lemonade," Summer replied, pulling open the refrigerator.

"Why don't you see if Faye wants some?" She pulled out a cutting board and knife.

"Oh, she seems pretty busy watching TV," Summer said. "Besides, she knows where it is if she gets thirsty." She poured herself a glass, returned the pitcher of lemonade to the fridge, and then gathered her bag.

"I suppose so," Mom replied, looking disappointed. "Well, dinner will be ready at about 5:00. Could you please set the table before then? We have to eat early tonight so I can get Faye to dance class."

"Sure, Mom," Summer said on her way out the door. She took the steps up to her room carefully so she wouldn't spill her lemonade, and then stopped at her sister Lisa's room. Sixteen-year-old Lisa laid on her stomach on her perfectly made bed, listening to her iPhone and writing something down in a notebook.

"Hey, Lisa, guess what? Tomorrow Mr. Camp is going to let us know who is singing the solo for our concert in a couple of weeks."

"Really," Lisa replied, not looking up from her notebook.

"I didn't try out. I mean, I know Cammie is a much better singer than I am, and then Pilar raised her hand to try out, so I knew I wouldn't have a chance..." Lisa's cell phoned buzzed and she snapped it up, waving at Summer to stop talking.

"Hello? Hey, Kayla..." Lisa said, turning her back to Summer. Summer sighed and went to the room she shared with Faye to start her homework. She closed the door and tossed her

9

tote on her bed. She scowled at Faye's side of the room, which was covered in horses and *Tangled* posters. She hated sharing a room with her baby sister. She would be lucky if she could get any homework done before Faye came in to bother her.

Summer kicked aside Faye's purple sneakers and sat down next to her tote. She blushed as she pulled out her math book, her thoughts returning to what she had been thinking about during the bus ride home.

Wes Jacobs had given Summer his phone number in math class that day. He said it was in case she needed help with their pre-algebra, which Summer thought was a little strange since she always aced the quizzes. Wes would know that, since they always swapped papers to grade in class. Maybe he wanted her to call him anyway...

Summer shook her head and opened the book to that day's lesson. It didn't matter that Wes was a popular soccer player at school. There was no way she was going to call him. If he wanted to talk to her on the phone, he'd have to have the courage to ask her for *her* number. Of course, then she'd be embarrassed when she had to look up in his clear blue eyes and tell him that she wasn't allowed to have a cell phone until she was in high school, so he'd have to call her home phone.

She tapped her pencil on her chin as she tried to think of what Maddie would say to smooth over that embarrassing situation. She then realized that she hadn't told Maddie about Wes' phone number. Summer hadn't wanted to tell her after she got off the bus because Cammie and Brittany would have gloated about being right, and then announced to the whole bus stop that Wes and Summer *liked* each other. She meant to tell Maddie after they had turned off on their street, but she'd been too distracted about the choir auditions and making sure Maddie was okay. She was about to go to the kitchen to call her when she remembered yet another rule: no phone calls until homework was done.

Summer kicked off her shoes, flopped on her back on her bed, and put her feet on the wall. She loved her parents, but sometimes she thought that they had way too many outdated rules. She got up, turned on her iPod, and got to her homework. The sooner she was done, the sooner she could call Maddie.

Chapter 2

"Where *is* Maddie?" Cammie huffed, impatient. "We're going to be late for choir." Summer shrugged and looked down the hall. The girls had decided to meet before going to choir, because Mr. Camp had posted the results of the audition outside the choir room door. They all wanted to look at it together.

Cammie had certainly dressed with care for the big announcement. She liked to dress in a funky, rock-star style. Today she was wearing dark skinny jeans and had layered two t-shirts: a long black one underneath and a purple one with a sparkly silver guitar painted on top. Her favorite black zip-up hoodie and a black studded choker completed the outfit. Her short hair spiked out in the back, and long bangs swept over her heavily made up eyes.

Summer looked down at her outfit. She liked to play it safe. She was wearing her worn-in jeans and a light blue baby-doll tunic sweater she had found at a garage sale this summer. She shifted her feet when she saw how dirty her black converse sneakers were. Her brown curly hair hung down to her shoulders. She was glad her mom had decided to let her wear mascara this year, and was still working to get permission to wear eye-liner.

Brittany stood next to Cammie, looking like a fashion plate. Her parents were both doctors and seemed to buy Brittany new clothes whenever they had to miss something because of work, which was a lot. Her jeans and peasant-style top were brand new and were very flattering on her short body. Her pale blond hair was long and held back with a wide headband.

"Sorry, guys! Mrs. Tile was standing outside her door, so I couldn't run through the hall," Maddie said, breathless as she walked quickly to the girls. Maddie wore her standard warm-up pants and grey hoodie. She had her hair up in a messy bun. Maddie didn't seem to care about looking in style, but it worked for her. Summer was sure she would just look like a slob if she tried to dress like Maddie, but Maddie pulled it off.

"This is it!" squealed Brittany. The four girls linked arms and rounded the corner to the choir room. A small group of students had paused at the bulletin board outside the room. The girls pressed in close behind them to read the sign.

"Pilar!" Cammie exclaimed in dismay. Her shoulders slumped and she dropped her book bag to the floor.

"I'm sorry, Cammie," Summer said softly. "Your audition was really good. I'm sure it was a hard choice for Mr. Camp."

"Yeah," Brittany said, picking up Cammie's bag and handing it to her. "Pilar probably brought him cookies or something, just to sweeten the deal."

Cammie smirked. "Or homemade tamales or whatever her grandma makes. Can I help it if my mom has a *life* and can't spend her time in the kitchen making goodies so I can get what I want at school?"

Brittany shrieked with laughter.

"Come on, Cammie," Maddie said. "Don't be like that. You were both good. She got it. There will be other solos. Maybe you can get Mr.

Camp to hold auditions again for the Christmas concert." Maddie lead the way into the classroom. "Besides, she brought in her grandma's tamales for a project in social studies, and they were really good." Cammie stuck her tongue out at Maddie's back.

The girls followed Maddie and filed into their seats in their respective sections, Cammie and Summer with the sopranos and Maddie and Brittany with the altos. Most of the kids were already in the room, including Pilar Sanchez, who quietly studied her music three seats over from Cammie.

"She probably has been here since Mr. Paulson opened the building at 7 a.m.," Cammie said under her breath. "I bet she helped Mr. Camp type up the announcement and pinned it to the board herself." Summer gave Cammie a small smile.

"You know, Cammie, he still needs strong voices in the choir during the solo part. Maybe he wanted you for that," Summer said.

Cammie let out a huge sigh as the bell rang to signal the start of class. Mr. Camp stepped up to the music stand positioned in front of the choir.

"Congratulations to Pilar Sanchez and Wes Jacobs," Mr. Camp said. "It's going to be a great fall program! We have two weeks left to polish these pieces, so let's get started with our warm ups." The choir stood and began to sing as the accompanist played scales on the piano.

Summer felt that familiar, unwanted flush heating up her face at the mention of Wes Jacob's name. She gave a sideways glance at Cammie to see if she'd noticed.

Summer didn't have to worry. Cammie was still fuming about the solo. She was singing the scales louder than necessary, as if to prove to Mr. Camp that she really could sing. Summer sighed to herself and turned her attention back to Mr. Camp.

#

At lunch, it was clear that Cammie was still in a bad mood.

"Look at her. Again with the music," Cammie pouted. Pilar sat at a table by herself, eating and reading. Cammie picked at the pepperoni on her slice of cafeteria pizza.

"I bet she can't even read words," Brittany said, handing Cammie a can of Dr. Pepper. "She can probably only read music."

"What can you do?" Summer asked, unwrapping her ham sandwich. "It's not like Mr. Camp will change his mind."

"I'm not worried about Mr. Camp. I'm worried about Pilar and that high horse she's on," Cammie retorted.

"High horse? Have you ever even talked to her?" Maddie asked, munching on some carrot sticks.

"Don't have to. I'm a good judge of character. I can tell," Cammie said.

The girls continued to giggle as Summer peeked over at Pilar.

Pilar ate her lunch and read her book, not paying attention to anything. She was actually a very pretty girl, with dark chocolate eyes and thick, wavy, black hair that reached her mid-back. She ate pasta out of a plastic container with a plastic fork. Pilar glanced up and saw Summer looking at her. She turned red and quickly dabbed at her mouth with a napkin, as if she were worried that there was sauce on her face. Summer snapped her head back to her friends.

"We should take her down a peg," Cammie said.

"Really? And how do you propose we do that?" Maddie asked dryly.

"We could mess up her hair on the night of the concert," Brittany said.

"No, that's dumb," Cammie said. "I know! We could trip her as we're walking on stage for the concert."

"What are you, seventh grade boys?" Maddie asked.

"You guys really aren't going to do anything are you?" Summer asked. "She's seriously just minding her own business."

"Yeah, because she thinks she's too good for us," Cammie demanded.

"I know! Let's spill something on her dress the night of the concert. She'll have to go on stage looking like a dork!" Brittany said with glee.

"Hmm, I could work with that," Cammie mused.

"Oh please. I'm about to spill my juice on you right now," Maddie said. "Actually, I have a better idea..." She tossed a grape at Cammie, making it land next to her pizza.

"Watch it, Ryland!" Cammie said, flicking a pepperoni in her direction.

"Food fight!" a boy yelled at the next table. Suddenly food was flying all over the cafeteria.

"Oh my gosh, guys. Run!" Cammie squealed. The four girls jumped up and ran out of the cafeteria, covering their heads against the flying sandwiches. Two teachers began blowing whistles and yelling for everyone to stop.

"Wow. I didn't see that coming," Maddie giggled.

"Hurry to the bathroom! Maybe no one knew we started it," Summer said. The girls scurried into the bathroom, laughing all the way.

Chapter 3

Two weeks passed by in a flurry of homework and school activities. It was the night of the Fall Concert and Summer was nervous. True, she didn't have the solo, but her parents and sisters were going to be there, and she wanted to sing her best. Especially since Lisa was coming. She was always so busy with her high school friends that taking out the time to come to Summer's middle school concert meant a lot to her.

The seventh grade Concert Choir hung out in the music room, waiting for the band and orchestra to finish their portion of the program. They were supposed to wait for Mr. Camp to come line them up so they could all file onto the stage together.

The choir room buzzed with chatting girls and laughing boys. Everyone was excited. It felt different being in the school after dark. Boys tossed paper airplanes in some kind of competition, while girls, sitting in clusters, touched up their lip gloss and picked invisible pieces of lint off their black skirts.

Summer and Maddie sat just inside the door of the choir room, chatting quietly. Wes Jacobs walked towards them.

"Hey, Summer," he said. "Ready for the concert?"

Summer smiled up at him. "Sure," she replied. "Of course, I don't have a solo like you, so I don't really have anything to worry about."

"Aw, it's no big deal." He sat down in the empty chair next to Summer.

"Hey, Wes."

"Oh, hey, Maddie," he replied, as if he just noticed her. A paper airplane pelted him in the chest, and he jumped out of his seat.

"See you later, Summer," he said as he headed for the corner hosting the airplane throwing contest.

"'See you later, Summer?'" Maddie asked, incredulous. "What was that all about?"

Summer felt the oh so familiar blush stain her cheeks. "I meant to tell you about that. He gave me his phone number."

21

"WHAT?!" shrieked Maddie.

Summer clutched Maddie's arm and tried to shush her. "It was a couple of weeks ago. Remember the bus ride home, when Cammie and Brittany were making fun of me for being so spacey? Well, I didn't want them to tease me about it, or to announce it to the world, so I didn't say anything. I was going to call you, but then..."

"Ugh, say no more," Maddie replied. "Those two can be ruthless. But I wish you had told me! Summer! He's so cute!"

Summer gave a small smile. "Yeah, well, if he wants to talk to me on the phone, he'll have to ask for my number."

Maddie laughed. "That's what I would say. Hey, where on Earth did Brittany and Cammie go? They left for the bathroom, like, ten minutes ago."

"They better hurry," Summer said, peeking out the door. "Mr. Camp is going to be here soon." Just then Brittany poked her head in the room.

"Hey guys, come here for a minute," she said, breathless with a twinkle in her eye.

"Where?" demanded Maddie. "Mr. Camp will be here any second, and we have to be ready to line up."

"Oh, just come on. The band still has two songs left." Maddie and Summer followed her out the door.

"Hold this, and don't drink it," she said to Summer, handing her a cup of punch.

"Where did you get this?" Summer asked.

"From the table in the lobby. It's supposed to be for the refreshments after the concert, but no one will mind," Brittany replied.

"What's it for? Where's mine?" Maddie asked.

"You don't need one. Oh, here they come. Act casual," Brittany said, bouncing up and down. They looked down the hall to see Cammie and Pilar coming toward them.

"Maybe you could just show me this part in the music I keep messing up," Cammie said to Pilar. "I know you can play it on the piano. I just don't want to ruin the concert."

"Oh, sure," Pilar said, looking pleased at being asked to help. Just as Cammie and Pilar reached the other girls, Cammie jumped back, and Brittany knocked into Summer from behind, causing her to dump the punch all over the front of Pilar's white blouse. Pilar, Summer, and Maddie all gasped.

"Oh no! Pilar, I'm so sorry," Summer cried.

"Oh my! What a mess! Come with me, Pilar. We'll clean that up in the bathroom," Cammie said, grabbing Pilar's arm.

Brittany muffled a giggle and ran beside them. "Yeah, some paper towels should do the trick." Summer and Maddie followed behind, shocked. Pilar's mouth hung open as she stared down at the red stain on her front.

Cammie pulled her forward. "Actually, there are paper towels in HERE," she said, swinging Pilar into the janitor's closet next to the girls' bathroom. Brittany quickly shut the door, then gave Cammie a high five. The two girls burst out laughing.

"Hey! Let me out of here!" Pilar shouted from the closet.

"What do you think you're doing?" Summer cried.

"This is so not funny," Maddie agreed, glaring at Cammie and Brittany.

"Oh relax. She'll be fine," Cammie said. "Maybe singing with a wet shirt will let her know she's not as important as she thinks she is."

"Did you see her face?" Brittany asked with glee. Summer reached for the doorknob. Then something horrible happened.

"Guys, it's locked!" Summer yelled.

"What?" Cammie said. "No it's not. I checked it after lunch today."

"Yeah, well, maybe someone locked it later, genius," Maddie said.

"Let me out! Please," Pilar begged.

"Um, we'll have to find someone," Summer called through the door. Just then they heard Mr. Camp call to them from the choir room.

"Come on, girls! Line up! We go on in two minutes!" he called. They looked at each other, then rushed down the hall and into the classroom.

"Where's Pilar?" Mr. Camp asked, once everyone had lined up.

"Um, she…" Summer started to say.

"She's not here. I haven't seen her," Cammie said.

"What?" Mr. Camp exclaimed. "I told you all to be in here and ready at 7:30. Well, we can't wait around for her. Cammie, can you sing the solo?"

25

"Of course, Mr. Camp," Cammie said, looking innocent.

"What about Pilar?" Summer hissed. Brittany elbowed her in the ribs. Mr. Camp sighed.

"Let's go, kids," he said, leading the way down the hall toward the auditorium. The band finished up their last number, a loud song with lots of drums. Only Summer and her friends heard the faint banging on the door of the janitor's closet behind them.

The choir filed on stage and sang their first two pieces without a hitch. Then Mr. Camp stepped to the microphone.

"Ladies and gentlemen, we have a slight program change. Cammie Dunn will sing the solo in this next piece, instead of Pilar Sanchez," he said. He then stepped back to the podium and cued the accompanist to begin. Cammie stepped confidently up to the mic.

Summer listened to the opening music and her stomach clenched with guilt. She caught a glimpse of Pilar's parents in the audience, looking baffled. They whispered to each other, and Pilar's mom got up and rushed out of the auditorium.

Summer snapped her eyes back to Mr. Camp just as he cued them to sing. Cammie was doing a wonderful job, but Summer felt that everything was wrong. She tried to focus on the song, but knew deep in her heart that this was not the kind of thing that someone could get away with.

Just then the song ended, and the crowd jumped to their feet in a standing ovation. Cammie beamed as Mr. Camp gestured to her to take a bow. She returned to her place in the choir flushing with pleasure.

Summer felt sick. Only one more song, and then she would have to find out what happened to Pilar.

Chapter 4

Summer couldn't believe it. The concert was over and the choir was back in the music room gathering their things so they could join their parents. Cammie and Brittany jumped up and down, squealing.

"You sounded s-o-o-o-o good!" Brittany yelled.

"I know!" Cammie replied. "I mean, thanks!"

Summer and Maddie stared at them in disbelief.

"Uh, hello? Do you girls even remember what happened before the concert?" Maddie asked, dumbfounded.

"What?" Cammie asked. "Oh yeah. I better go tell someone something."

Brittany turned to her, suddenly worried. "What are you going to tell them? You'll get in trouble."

"No I won't. I'll just tell the janitor or someone that I think Pilar got locked in the closet by mistake. That's what happened anyway."

"Yeah, after *you* pushed her in!" Maddie said.

"Stop being dramatic. It was an accident. I didn't lock her in there on purpose, so I can't get in trouble for something I didn't do," Cammie said, tossing her head and marching out the door with Brittany hot on her heels.

Summer wiped her sweaty hands on her skirt. She slowly picked up her coat.

"I'd better go find my parents," she said softly. "They'll be wondering where I am."

"Yeah, me too," Maddie said. "This is not going to be good, you know."

"It's not your fault. I was holding the punch."

Summer and Maddie walked out the door and down the hall to the lobby where cookies and punch had been set out. She scanned the crowded area for her family.

"Summer! Over here!" Faye waved wildly across the room. Summer turned beet red as she glanced around to see if anyone noticed her noisy baby sister. Maddie gave her a quick squeeze on the arm before joining her parents at the cookie table.

"Great concert, Summer!" Mom exclaimed, giving her a hug.

"Nice job, Sweet Thing," her dad echoed.

"Thanks," Summer said, swallowing hard. "Where's Lisa?"

"Oh, she saw someone from school. She's over by the door," Mom replied. "How about some cookies?"

"Can we just go?" Summer said. "I'm tired and not that hungry."

"I am! I wanted cookies. You said, Mom!" Faye whined.

"Don't worry, honey, you can go get cookies," Mom said.

"I'll take her," Dad said. "Come on, Sprout. It'll be a date." Faye giggled as she grabbed his hand. They pushed their way through the crowd toward the cookie table.

"What's wrong?" Mom asked. "You look pale. Are you sick?"

"No," Summer replied. "Like I said, I'm just tired." Just then she saw Pilar and her parents enter the lobby with the janitor. Cammie and Brittany were on the other side of the room getting big hugs from their parents. Maddie had already left.

Suddenly Pilar made eye contact with Summer. Her face was puffy and red, and her parents looked really upset. Summer looked away, relieved that her dad and Faye were back.

"We're all set! Let's blow this pop stand," Dad said with a twinkle in his eye. Summer groaned. "Dad, don't be so corny. Someone might hear you," she said.

"Well, they'll hear this: LISA! WE'RE OUT!" he boomed. Lisa scowled in their direction and said goodbye to her friend.

"Jeez, Dad," Lisa said as the McKidd family trouped out the door. "Next time text. It'll be just as fast."

"I don't know how to type on those tiny buttons," Dad replied. "Besides, I like the sound of my own voice." Mom laughed as Summer and Lisa exchanged an eye roll.

Once at the van, the family piled into their usual seats, with Faye in the back and Lisa and Summer in the two seats in the middle.

"I could have driven myself, you know," Lisa informed her parents. She had gotten her driver's license earlier that fall and was eager to drive everywhere.

"And miss out on family time? I don't think so," Dad said as he guided the van out of the parking lot.

"Cammie did a great job with that solo, don't you think Summer?" Mom asked. Summer's palms began to sweat again.

"Yeah, she did great," Summer said. "Cammie is one of the best singers in the choir."

"What happened to that Pilar girl?" Lisa asked. "Why did Mr. Camp make the switch?"

"I thought that was strange, too," Mom said.

Summer frantically tried to think of what to say. Should she tell her parents what happened? *She* wasn't the one who locked Pilar in the closet, so there was nothing to hide. They would probably understand when she told them that Brittany had been the one to hand her the punch, and then knock into Summer from behind. But then they would want to know why Summer hadn't said anything. She'd probably get a lecture about not finding an adult when she got into trouble.

"Hello? Summer?" Lisa said.

"Pilar wasn't there when it was time for us to line up," Summer said quickly, opting for part of the truth. "We didn't have time to go get her, so Mr. Camp asked Cammie to sing instead." There. All of that was absolutely true.

"Oh. Well, Cammie did very nice, but it's too bad about Pilar. I saw her parents there. They must have been really disappointed," Mom said.

"Did you ever find out what happened to Pilar?" Dad asked.

"Um, maybe she got nervous or something," Summer replied. She turned and looked out the window. Her family bought the story!

"Well, tomorrow's Friday," Dad said. "What are our plans for the weekend?"

"Oh the usual cleaning on Saturday," Mom replied.

"I want to go to the zoo," Faye announced.

"On a Saturday? It'll be jam-packed, Faye," Mom said. "Maybe we can do something else. Like rent a movie."

"I wanted to go to the mall on Saturday," Lisa said. "Summer, you could come if you want."

"Really?" Summer said, snapping forward in her seat. "Of course!" Lisa *rarely* asked if Summer wanted to hang out.

"Sounds like a good plan," Mom said. "As long as you both are done with your homework *and* your chores."

"I will be!" Summer said.

"We know, we know," Lisa said.

"What am *I* supposed to do this weekend if all you girls are ditching me?" Dad moaned.

"I'm sure you'll find something to do, Dear," Mom replied with a smile. They all knew that Dad was perfectly happy to stay at home by himself watching golf or reading the paper.

Summer smiled as they pulled into the driveway. She was so excited about the weekend plans that she forgot all about the trouble at the concert. She couldn't wait to tell the girls about going to the mall with Lisa. She began planning her outfit for school the next day as she walked inside and headed to her room.

Chapter 5

"See you in choir!" Summer called to her friends as she turned down the hall toward her homeroom. The girls had bounced in their seats during the bus ride to school. Cammie was still excited about the concert, Brittany was still excited for her, Maddie was excited that it was Friday, and Summer was excited about going to the mall with Lisa. Summer didn't have homeroom with any of them, so she walked to class by herself.

"Hey Summer," said a smooth voice. Summer looked behind her to see Wes trotting down the hall.

"Hey, Wes," she replied, hugging her tote closer to her body.

"The concert went well, don't you think?" he asked, falling into step beside her. She caught a strong whiff of his cologne. She immediately decided it was her favorite cologne of all time.

"Yeah," she said. "You did a great job with the solo."

"Thanks." He flashed a smile. They reached the door to homeroom. Their assigned seats were on opposite sides of the classroom.

"Well, see you in choir," Wes said, taking off for his corner. Summer smiled at him and headed for her seat.

"Miss McKidd?" Mrs. Pale, her homeroom teacher, said. Summer turned and headed for the teacher's desk.

"Good morning, Mrs. Pale."

"Good morning. Mrs. Dobson has requested your presence immediately. You may go there now," she said, looking Summer in the eye. Summer's heart dropped. All the good feelings she had fluttered away like a startled butterfly. The principal's office!

"Yes, ma'am," Summer said quietly. She quickly headed out the door. The bell rang just as she was leaving and the hallways emptied in a flash. Summer felt naughty as she walked down the halls while everyone else was in class. She had never been called to the principal's office before. She mentally chastised herself for forgetting all about the trouble from last night. She took a big breath and opened the door to the office.

"Mrs. Dobson asked for me," Summer told the secretary.

"Name?" the secretary asked.

"Summer McKidd," Summer replied, feeling miserable. The secretary's eyes snapped up from the computer.

"Sit down over there," she said softly. She rose from her chair and tapped on the principal's door before slipping inside. Summer was glad to sit. She didn't think her legs could hold her much longer. The hall door opened and Cammie, Brittany, and Maddie filed in. They all looked scared.

"I told you this would be bad," Maddie said to Summer, plopping in the seat next to her.

"And I told *you* this wasn't our fault because it was an accident," Cammie said. She sat down and crossed her legs, slumping down the chair. Mrs. Dobson's door opened and the principal herself stepped out. She was a tall lady with short brown hair and kind eyes. Today her eyes looked gravely serious.

"Summer? I'll talk to you first since you arrived first. The rest of you are expected to sit silently until I call you," she said firmly. Summer stood as the other three girls nodded and looked at their feet. Mrs. Dobson opened the door wider for Summer to enter, then closed the door gently behind them.

"Have a seat, Summer," Mrs. Dobson said, pointing to one of two chairs in front of her desk. Summer sat and was surprised to see Mrs. Dobson sit in the other one, rather than going back behind the desk.

"I think I'd like you to tell me what happened," she said. Summer decided to not even pretend to not know what Mrs. Dobson was talking about. She was aware that she was still hugging her tote bag as she spilled the whole story, her eyes filling with tears.

"I promise I didn't know what Cammie had planned," Summer said when she finished. "But I *was* holding the cup of punch." A tear trickled down her cheek, and Mrs. Dobson handed her a tissue.

"I believe you," Mrs. Dobson said. "I'm not going to sugar-coat it, Summer, but what happened was awful. I see your biggest crime as not telling Mr. Camp what happened right before the concert."

"I know," Summer replied. "It's just that he was telling us that it was time to go, and we didn't think there was time to explain and then find someone to help..."

"There is *always* time to help someone in trouble," Mrs. Dobson said. "Pilar's parents were really upset, and I've promised that I will take care of this. Normal protocol for this kind of hazing is a three-day suspension. Pilar did tell us her version of the story and your stories match. Since you weren't involved in the planning, I'm only suspending you for today. It will go on your record, though. I've already called your parents. They should be here any minute to pick you up." Summer gasped, then nodded.

"Summer," Mrs. Dobson said, leaning closer, "You should never be afraid to do what's right, including asking an adult for help when you know there's trouble. You may get into a little trouble at the time, but it can prevent things from becoming a lot worse."

"I'm so sorry!" Summer cried. "I just feel so bad for Pilar. I know her parents were probably so happy she was singing the solo, and then she didn't even get to do it."

"It's good to have that kind of compassion. Now go wait in the office for your parents. And please do not speak to the other girls. We'll see you Monday."

"Yes ma'am," Summer said, wiping her nose with the tissue. She slipped out into the office without looking at the other girls.

"Maddie?" Mrs. Dobson called. Maddie stood looking stricken and hurried into the office. Summer sat in the chair furthest away from Cammie and Brittany.

"Summer," Cammie hissed. "What did you say in there?"

"Girls, no talking," the secretary said.

Summer avoided eye contact with everybody. It seemed like she waited hours, but really her mom walked in the office door about five minutes later.

"Summer," she said, looking solemn. The secretary nodded at them and handed Mom a slip of paper.

"You can go," she said. Mom turned around and walked out the door, leaving Summer to follow. Summer walked slowly behind her all the way out to the car.

Chapter 6

The car ride home was awful. Mom didn't say a word, and she kept the radio off. Summer sat in the front seat, staring out the window and mindlessly twirling a strand of hair around and around her finger. She wondered if Cammie would be mad at her for what she told Mrs. Dobson. She wondered what would happen to the other girls. She wondered if everyone in school knew what they did. And most of all, she wondered what was going to happen to her once she got home.

All too soon Mom pulled the van into the garage, turned off the engine, and sat with her hands in her lap. Summer reached for the door handle.

"Your father will be home at lunch," Mom said. "Please go to your room until then." Summer swallowed hard. Whenever she was in trouble, Mom said things like "your father" instead of "Dad." She nodded, then opened the door and hurried into the house.

She fled to her room, shut the door, and flopped on the bed. She truly felt awful about everything that happened. How would she explain this to her parents? Would they believe her when she said it wasn't her fault? And then there was Pilar. Pilar hadn't done anything to her or her friends, and they ruined her big night.

Summer went over to her desk and pulled out some notebook paper. She had to write a note to Pilar to apologize. She worked on the note for hours, writing and rewriting, until she heard Dad come home. She looked at the clock, surprised at the time.

"Summer? Lunch is ready," Mom called. Summer slowly went downstairs and found Mom and Dad sitting at the table with grilled cheese sandwiches and tomato soup. She sat at the place set for her and stared at her hands folded in her lap.

"I'll pray," Dad said. "Lord, thank you for this food. Give us wisdom, patience, and grace as we talk today. Amen."

Mom and Dad both started eating their sandwiches. Summer wasn't feeling hungry. She took a small sip of tomato soup, wincing as it burned her tongue. After a few minutes of silence, her mom was the first to speak.

"Why didn't you say anything?"

"I-I-I knew you'd be disappointed. And the concert was over, and I saw Pilar standing with her parents so I knew she was okay," Summer began.

"We need to hear the whole story, honey," Dad said. So once again, Summer gave every detail she could think of, emphasizing the part that she didn't know what was going on and that Brittany had been the one to hand her the punch.

"It may not have been your idea, but you were responsible for your actions from the moment you were handed that punch," Dad said. "You should have told Mr. Camp where Pilar was."

"I know that now," Summer replied.

"I think it's kind of amazing you were only suspended for one day," Mom said. "Mrs. Dobson said over the phone that the school has a zero tolerance policy for this kind of bullying."

"We weren't bullying," Summer said.

"*You* might not have been, but Cammie and Brittany were," Dad said firmly. "You need to be aware of what your friends are doing." Summer stared down at her plate.

"Let's talk punishment," Mom said. Summer looked up quickly.

"Punishment? You mean *besides* being suspended?" Summer squeaked.

"This is serious, Summer. I can tell by that question that you really aren't aware of how serious it is."

"I think being grounded for two weeks is fair," Dad said. "No extra activities, no phone calls, no email."

Grounded! That would mean no mall with Lisa. Summer tried to hold back the tears, but they squeezed out. Who knew when Lisa would ask her to go to the mall again?

"I also think you need to do a little community service," Dad continued. "It'll teach you to be aware of other people."

"Community service?" Summer said. "Like what? Picking up trash?"

"No," Mom said. "Nursery duty. They are always looking for volunteers in the nursery. I called the nursery director this morning, and she said that you could help with the toddlers. There will be a couple adults in there as well, of course. You'll start on Sunday during the first service."

"But we go to the second service," Summer said.

"I will drive you over in time for the second. After nursery, you can come and sit with us. No sitting with the youth group while you're grounded," Dad said. First no mall with Lisa, and now no sitting with the youth group. The youth *always* sat together during church. Everyone would see her sitting by her parents and know that she was in trouble.

"I, I, um, how long do I have to work in the nursery?" Summer asked, hoping they were only making her work during her grounding.

"At least until the end of the year," Mom said. The end of the year! It was mid-October; that meant two and half months! Summer took a bit of her sandwich and found that she wasn't hungry at all.

"May I be excused please?" Summer asked.

"You didn't eat much," Mom said.

"I'm not that hungry."

"Okay, then. Don't snack too close to dinner."

Summer stood and walked slowly back to her room. She closed the door and leaned against it. Tears began streaming down her face.

This wasn't fair! It wasn't even her idea. She had told Cammie and Brittany that it wasn't funny. The only thing she did wrong was not tell Mr. Camp where Pilar was. Now she was suspended, grounded, and sentenced to nursery duty. Maybe she *should* have been a part of the planning. Then the punishment would fit the crime. Being suspended should have been enough for her parents.

They were just too strict! She bet that Maddie's parents wouldn't be so hard. No way would they ground her from volleyball. Brittany's parents were doctors and worked all the time, so even if they grounded Brittany, she could still do whatever she wanted at home. Cammie's parents were jokesters themselves; they would probably spend the weekend laughing at what Cammie did and praising her for her excellent solo.

Maybe Cammie was right. Maybe Pilar really *was* trouble. If she hadn't tattled, then Summer wouldn't be in this position. Summer stomped over to her desk and picked up the apology letter. She ripped it up and hurled the pieces into the trash can. One of Faye's stuffed horses sat on the floor; Summer kicked it under Faye's bed.

She flopped once more on her bed, breathing hard. She grabbed her journal and began to write quick, angry, sloppy words. After about 20 minutes, Summer was spent. She rolled on her side and stared at the wall. She might as well start counting down the days to when her grounding was over.

She'd have to wait until Monday to find out what happened to her friends. She sighed. A whole weekend stuck at home, probably with Faye bugging her to play horses or something. And Sunday she'd have to start working in the nursery. Was it just that morning when she had been so excited about the weekend? Now Summer had nothing to be excited about. It was going to be the longest weekend of her life.

Chapter 7

By Sunday, Summer was actually glad to have nursery duty. She was tired of being cooped up in the house with only Faye and her parents for company. Lisa had gone to the mall without her on Saturday and then had spent the evening at her friend's house. Summer was ready for some interaction with other people, even if those other people were screaming toddlers.

She made her way to the nursery and poked her head in the toddler class. There were five toddlers already in there. Two of them were crying. Summer sighed and walked in to greet the teacher.

"I'm Summer McKidd. I'm supposed to be helping," Summer told the petite, plump woman who was trying to comfort one of the criers.

"Oh Summer, I'm so glad you're here," she said. "I'm Cathy Thomas. We've needed help for so long! Thank you for coming." The crier she held stopped crying and stared at Summer. "We usually have 12 or 15 toddlers in here this hour, so it can get kind of crazy!"

"Um, what do I do?" Summer asked. She hoped Mrs. Thomas wouldn't find out that she wasn't there out of the goodness of her heart; that she was forced to be there by her strict parents.

"Oh, just play with the kids! Keep the peace if a fight breaks out. Betty Lyons is the other adult helper and she and I will do story time in about 30 minutes. We'll have a snack, and by the time that gets cleaned up, the parents are usually coming to pick up their kiddos." Mrs. Thomas put the toddler down and went over to welcome another toddler who was being dropped off.

Summer turned around and saw three of the kids staring at her. She crouched down to their level.

"Hi, guys. Want to play?" Two of them continued to stare, but one little girl picked up a doll and brought it to Summer. She handed Summer the doll, then raised her arms to be picked up. Summer checked the name tag on the back of the girl's shirt.

"Hi Lily," she said. "We'll have fun today." Lily smiled and began to chatter about the doll.

"YOU." Summer heard an angry voice behind her and whirled around to see Pilar Sanchez glaring at her. She almost dropped Lily.

"Pilar! What are you doing here?" Summer cried without thinking.

"What am *I* doing here? This is my class. I've helped out in here all year," she replied. "What are *you* doing here?"

"Oh, um, I'm helping here, too, for a while," Summer said.

"Great," Pilar muttered. Pilar marched over to the toy box and began pulling out some toy trucks. Three little boys ran over, each yelling about their favorite truck.

Summer sat down in a tiny chair meant for toddlers, still clutching Lily. Lily squirmed to be let down, and Summer let her go. *Pilar* worked in this class? Summer didn't even know that Pilar went to her church! How was she supposed to face Pilar each Sunday after what she did? It was going to be pretty easy to avoid her at school, but church was a whole different story.

Just then three more toddlers were dropped off by their parents. They weren't happy about it. Summer shifted her focus to the crying kids, trying to think of ways to calm them down. Pilar came over and swung one little girl into her arms. She began to sing a silly song, bouncing around the room with the girl. The little girl immediately switched from crying to giggling. A couple of other toddlers began dancing behind Pilar, forming a funny looking conga line. The kid Summer was trying to comfort ran over to join the dance party. Soon all the kids were shrieking with joy.

"If you want to know what to do, just watch Pilar," Mrs. Thomas said. "That girl is a wonder with this age group." Summer couldn't help but laugh at the whole group and their antics.

The rest of the hour sailed by. Summer and Pilar were very busy trying to keep the kids calm during story time, and snack time ended up being one mess after another. Before Summer knew it the hour was over and parents lined up to pick up their kids.

The kids saw the line of parents and were all yelling, "Mommy! Daddy!"

Soon the room was empty, and Pilar and Summer were setting the room back to rights for the second service.

"You're really good with the kids," Summer said. Pilar shrugged.

"I have seven cousins under the age of six. I've always been the one in charge of entertaining them."

"Well, I wouldn't have known what to do if you weren't here." Pilar gave Summer a shy smile. She turned and headed for the door. Summer knew that this was her chance to apologize.

"Pilar, wait!" She ran over to the door. "I am so sorry about what happened at the concert. It wasn't funny, and it definitely wasn't fair."

"Thanks, Summer. I knew it wasn't your fault."

"Yeah, but I should have told Mr. Camp that you were locked in the closet. I'm so so sorry."

"Don't worry about it. I forgive you." Pilar smiled a real smile at Summer and left the classroom.

Summer's heart felt light as she made her way into the main auditorium for the second service. She headed to where her parents were seated on the opposite side of the room from the youth group. She tried not to look over there, worried that if anyone saw her she would feel embarrassed and lose the good feeling she had over settling things with Pilar.

"Hi Honey," Mom said. "How were the kids?"

"Fine actually," Summer replied. "Did you know that Pilar Sanchez works in that class?"

"What?" Mom said, looking shocked. "No! Oh dear. How did that go?"

"Really well. She is great with kids. I even apologized about what happened."

"That's wonderful. I'm proud of you, Summer."

"You're still grounded, though," Dad said from the other side of Mom.

"I know," Summer said. "I understand."

The worship team began playing the first song, and everyone stopped their conversations and stood up to sing. Summer felt that her punishment was almost over. Yes, she was still grounded, but that would end soon, and maybe working the nursery wasn't so bad after all. It was really fun to play with Pilar and the kids.

Summer gave a sideways glance at her parents. Maybe she shouldn't let on that working in the nursery was going to be fun.

She wouldn't want them thinking that they needed to punish her in a different way. It felt good to know that this part of her punishment was actually going to be fun.

Chapter 8

On Monday morning, Summer arrived at the bus stop a little earlier than usual. She was the first one there. She was anxious to see her friends, since she hadn't seen or talked to any of them since they were all in the principal's office. She'd had to listen to a big lecture from her dad the night before about not following the crowd, and picking your friends wisely. She had nodded in all the right places, but now just really wanted to talk to Maddie, Cammie, and Brittany.

"Summer!" Maddie called as she raced toward her.

"Maddie!" Summer bounced up and down, waving. Maddie slammed into Summer with a huge hug, almost toppling them both into the grass.

"What happened to you?" Summer asked.

"I was suspended just for Friday, since I didn't really do anything," Maddie said. "And my parents grounded me from the phone and Internet for a week."

"Me too! I mean, I was only suspended for Friday, and I'm grounded for two weeks. From everything, though. Phone, Internet, *and* extra activities."

"Bummer! At least we get to see each other now." Maddie grabbed Summer in another hug, as if they hadn't seen each other in years.

"Oh, and I guess I'm sentenced to nursery duty at church," Summer said. She hadn't decided whether or not to tell the girls that Pilar helped in her class, too.

"Man! Don't take this the wrong way, but I'm so glad I don't have your parents."

"Ugh, I know. What happened to Cammie and Brittany? Any idea?"

"I guess we'll find out today," Maddie said. "Mrs. Dobson seemed like it was a big deal that I was only getting suspended for one day, so something tells me Cammie and Brittany may have gotten it worse."

"Do you think everyone at school knows?" Summer asked, lowering her voice.

"Probably." Maddie shifted her bag from one shoulder to the other. "You know how everyone likes to talk."

More students began to arrive at the bus stop, and Summer and Maddie fell silent. They were watching to see if anyone was looking at them differently.

Soon the bus came, and still no sign of Cammie or Brittany.

"I guess that answers our question," Maddie said. "I wonder how long they were suspended."

The bus ride went quickly, with Summer and Maddie both speculating what happened to their friends. Once at school, the girls gave each other another quick hug and headed off for their homerooms. Summer walked faster than normal. She didn't want to stop and talk to anyone.

She was about to turn the corner for the final stretch of hall when she heard a familiar "Hey, Summer!" She sighed and slowly turned around.

"Summer! What happened to you?" Wes asked, a little out of breath from jogging to catch up with her.

"Um, I, well, what have you heard?" Summer stammered.

"All I know is there was a prank involving five girls at the concert, and all of a sudden you weren't at school that day. Was it you?"

"Kind of. It wasn't my fault," Summer said, looking at her shoes.

"Well, since you, Maddie, Cammie, and Brittany weren't in choir, I kind of figured it was you guys. Mr. Camp gave us a huge lecture about pranks. Actually, all our teachers did. In every class."

"Oh. Sorry about that."

"Hey, I know the kind of people Cammie and Brittany are. Don't worry about it. You were just in the wrong place at the wrong time, right?"

"Right." Summer smiled up at Wes. It felt like he really understood. "I was suspended for one day, and I'm grounded for two weeks," she felt free to tell him.

"Bummer," he said. "Well, I'm glad you're back. See you later."

They arrived at the classroom. Wes went and sat down at his desk. Summer slowly sat down in hers, wondering how Mrs. Pale was going to treat her. Summer was bracing herself for looks of disapproval, but none came. In fact, no one but Wes even acknowledged what had happened.

With each hour, Summer felt like she could breathe easier. She hated being in trouble, and she didn't like being the center of attention, either. She only had to face choir.

When they got to the choir room, Mr. Camp pulled Summer and Maddie aside.

"Girls, I want you know that both Pilar and Mrs. Dobson have told me about the situation. I feel you two have been punished enough and trust you will come to me if any trouble like this ever happens again."

"Yes, sir," they both said.

"Good. Choir only works best when everyone works together as a team. I told the class on Friday, and I'll tell you now that I'll be reevaluating how I choose soloists. It shouldn't create that kind of competition. Now, go to your seats. Glad to have you back."

"Thanks, Mr. Camp," Maddie said, looking relieved. She gave Summer a small smile before heading to her section. Summer sat with the sopranos, a few chairs away from Pilar, who had her nose buried in some music. Summer didn't know if she should give Pilar space or say, "Hi."

After a few minutes of trying to weigh pros and cons, she chose the latter.

"Hey, Pilar," Summer said. Pilar looked up, surprised that someone was talking to her.

"Oh, hi, Summer," she said, shyly. She looked back at her music.

Summer was a little surprised. Pilar hadn't been shy at all when they were in the nursery. In fact, she had acted like she was in charge. She didn't have time to think about it, though. Choir was starting and Summer wanted to give it her full attention.

#

Later at lunch, Summer and Maddie still felt like everyone was looking at them. Without Cammie and Brittany there with them, they were sure they stuck out like losers.

"I wish the other girls were here," Maddie said around a mouthful of food. "I feel like our table is empty without them. Plus, they're always good for a laugh."

Summer smiled. "Did anyone say anything to you today?"

"Just Mr. Camp. You?"

"Well, um, Wes Jacobs asked what happened. He said that everyone got lectures about pranks in every class, so I guess everyone knows that a prank happened."

"Wes Jacobs noticed you were gone? That's a good sign." Maddie grinned. Summer blushed.

"Yeah, well, we have homeroom together, so he saw me come to school on Friday, and then I wasn't there for choir..."

"Don't explain," Maddie said, grabbing Summer's arm. "I shouldn't tease you. I know how things are between you two."

"No, it's okay," Summer said quickly. She was glad Maddie understood. It was exciting to share something like that with her. The girls continued to chat as they ate their lunch.

As Summer gathered her trash at the end of the lunch period, she looked over and saw Pilar eating by herself. She was reading a book. Summer was disappointed that she hadn't thought to ask her eat lunch with them. The truth was, she just forgot about her.

Throughout the day, whenever she saw Pilar around school, she tried to remember why Cammie and Brittany made fun of her so much.

Summer decided it wasn't her business as she rode the bus home that day. Maddie had volleyball practice, so Summer sat by herself. She missed Cammie and Brittany. It was always better to have friends on the bus. Summer felt self-conscious when she was by herself, like the other kids were looking at her and thinking she was a loser. She quickly walked home and tried to enter her house as quietly as she could.

"Hi, Summer!" Faye called from her usual spot on the couch. "Are you done being suspended?"

"*Yes*, Faye. That's why I went to school today."

"Oh yeah. Do you want to watch TV with me?"

"I suppose," Summer sighed. If she didn't watch for a little while, Faye would probably bug her all night. Faye bounced up and down.

"You can pick the show," she said, handing over the remote. Summer smiled at Faye and turned the channel.

Chapter 9

Cammie and Brittany didn't show up at the bus stop until Wednesday. There was a lot of squealing and jumping when the four girls were finally together again.

"Oh. My. Word. Can you *believe* we were suspended for so long?" Cammie wailed.

"I thought I was going to die not talking to you guys!" Brittany said. "Plus I was going crazy in that house!"

"I tried emailing you all," Cammie said.

"Yeah, we were both grounded from the Internet," Maddie said.

"That's awful!" Brittany said. "What did you do while you were home?"

"Um, well, we were only suspended on Friday, so..." Summer started.

"*WHAT?*" Cammie shrieked. "Why?"

"Well, since we didn't plan the prank, Mrs. Dobson only suspended us for one day," Maddie said.

"That is *so* not fair! I told them it wasn't our plan to lock her in the closet!" Cammie fumed.

"Well, I got grounded from everything for two weeks, and I have to work in the nursery at church until at least Christmas," Summer said, trying to show Cammie that she was indeed punished enough.

"Oh. Really?" Cammie said, looking hopeful.

"Yeah. *And* Pilar works in the class I work in, so I have to spend an hour with her every Sunday," Summer said, knowing how Cammie would react.

"That's terrible!" Brittany said. "How can you stand being in there with her?"

"Seriously," Cammie said. "I was only suspended for three days. My parents thought that was punishment enough. At least I don't have to work with *Pee*-lar!"

Brittany giggled, then apologized. Maddie was staring at Summer.

"You didn't tell me she was in there," she said quietly. She looked hurt. Summer grabbed her arm and pulled her away from the giggling Cammie and Brittany.

"It's not really that big a deal. She's actually kind of nice. I just didn't want Cammie to feel bad for being suspended longer than us, and I knew she'd think it was awful that I have to spend time with Pilar."

"Well, I guess I'd tell her anything too to keep her from being mad at *me,*" Maddie said.

"You *definitely* got it the worst!" Cammie said when they turned around. "At least my punishment is over! How can you stand working with her?"

"Oh, um, the hour goes by fast," Summer said. It was partly true. Summer didn't want to spend any energy trying to convince Cammie that Pilar was really a fun person. Plus, it would make Cammie cranky, and Summer didn't want her friends to be cranky on their first day back.

Everything was back to normal at school. Cammie made a big deal about "being free" and told everyone who would listen how it wasn't her fault. Some of the kids treated her like a local celebrity, asking again and again about what happened the night of the concert. Cammie was glad to tell them.

Summer became uncomfortable in choir. Mr. Camp hadn't come in yet. Cammie was standing in the soprano section, loudly recounting the concert story again for a crowd of kids. Pilar sat in her usual spot, looking down at her music. Summer knew she could hear every word.

"You should have seen the look on Pilar's face when she saw the punch on her shirt!" Cammie said. "She probably thought it was blood or something."

The kids roared with laughter.

"Anyway, we pushed her in the janitor's closet as a joke, and the door turned out to be locked. I didn't know it was going to be locked! Then Mr. Camp was calling us, and there was no time to explain. I didn't know he was going to ask me to sing the solo!" Several kids nodded in agreement and started discussing the reasons for not telling Mr. Camp.

Summer slumped down in her seat and looked over at Pilar. Pilar wiped her hand across her face and sighed. Was she crying? Summer leaned over to get a better look when Mr. Camp walked in.

"In your seats, everyone," he commanded. The crowd around Cammie quickly dispersed. She sat down. Mr. Camp frowned at them as he stood behind his music stand in front of the choir.

"I've thought about it, and I've decided I'm not going to change how I pick my soloists," Mr. Camp told the group. "The system is good. Everyone learns the solo. Everyone who wants to try out can. You guys need to learn to respect my decisions. I know I have more than one good soloist in here, and I will do my best to give everyone a chance. But you have to learn that you won't always be the one to get picked. This is as basic as kindergarten folks; everyone takes turns." As he finished his speech, he looked directly at Cammie. Cammie had the decency to squirm in her seat.

"It's time to start working on music for the Christmas program," Mr. Camp went on. "Pilar will be singing the solo in one of the songs, since, sadly, she missed the performance last week. We'll hold our regular auditions for the boy's solo." With that, he asked everyone to stand up and motioned for the accompanist to begin the warm up scales.

Cammie stood up and began singing loudly. She looked determined to once again prove what a great singer she was.

Summer glanced over at Pilar while she sang. Pilar stared straight at Mr. Camp while she sang her scales. Her face looked clear and dry. Maybe she hadn't been crying.

Summer decided not to worry about Pilar. Everything that had happened was over. Her friends were all back together and everything was back to normal. Cammie was just a jokester; Summer knew that. She always had been. Surely Pilar knew that it was just a joke that went horribly wrong. Anyway, Summer had apologized, and Pilar had forgiven her. Forgiveness meant that you don't have to worry about whatever happened anymore, right?

Summer stood up a little straighter and sang a little louder. Her life was back to normal. Or, at least it would be at the end of her two-week grounding.

Chapter 10

On Sunday, Summer was glad when it was time for nursery. Once again she was tired of being at home with just her family for company. Lisa had made plans for the weekend and wasn't around much, and Faye had been constantly begging for Summer to play on the Wii with her. Summer tried her best to be patient with Faye, but she had her limits. She was ready to spend an hour with fun, crazy toddlers and Pilar.

Pilar was already in the nursery when Summer arrived. She set up dolls in a little circle.

"Hi, Pilar!" Summer called as she walked in.

"Hey, Summer," Pilar replied, smiling over her shoulder. "I thought the little girls might like to have a tea party today. Think you can keep the boys from knocking everything over?"

"Oh, um, I guess. How do I do that?"

"Just set out trucks and cars. Maybe organize a car race, or make up a race course on the other side of the room."

"Wow. Where do you come up with this stuff?" Summer was amazed that Pilar could effortlessly rattle off ideas to keep the little ones occupied.

"I don't know. It just comes to me." Pilar looked shy, but a little proud about her ideas.

After the nursery hour was over, Summer and Pilar began talking about school as they cleaned up the room.

"Everyone knows Wes Jacobs likes you, Summer," Pilar told her.

"What? What do you mean 'everybody'?"

"Oh please. We all see how he pays special attention to you in math, and how he is always talking to you on the way to homeroom." Pilar grinned when Summer blushed.

"Well, we're just friends. I haven't even given him my phone number or anything."

"Has he asked for it?"

"Um, no. He gave me his, but my mom always says that the guy should do the calling. Is that old-school?"

"No way! He should definitely be the one to ask for it," Pilar said. Summer smiled. She had never talked to anyone besides Maddie about Wes before, and it was nice to have someone else's point of view.

"Hey, how come I've never seen you at youth group?" Summer asked.

"Oh, well, my family only has one car, and my dad has to work on Friday nights," Pilar replied, looking at her shoes.

"Oh. Well, if you ever want a ride, let me know," Summer offered. "Youth group is really fun. My sister Lisa always drives us. I'm sure we could swing by and pick you up sometime."

"Wow. Really? Okay, sure! I'd love to come!"

"Oh wait. Um, would it be okay if we came and got you next week? I'm kind of still grounded," Summer said, embarrassed that she had to take back her invitation.

"Of course. Grounded, huh? What did you do?" Pilar asked.

"Uh, well, you know, the concert and everything..." Summer said.

"Oh." Pilar turned bright red. "Next week would be great. I suppose I should ask my parents anyway. Thanks for inviting me."

"Sure." Summer grinned at Pilar as they walked down the hall toward the auditorium.

#

On the way home from church, Summer turned to Lisa.

"Hey, Lisa. Could we start picking up Pilar on the way to youth group? She's never been because her family only has one car, and her dad has to work on Friday nights, so she has no way to get there."

"I guess," Lisa said, wrinkling her nose. "When did I become the taxi driver for junior high kids?"

"The moment you got your license," Dad piped in.

"Wait," Mom said. "There are laws about teenage drivers not driving with other kids in their car. I'm not sure this will work. Lisa is only allowed to drive family."

"What? Oh no! I've already told Pilar we could take her!" Summer felt horrible. First she locked Pilar in a closet, then she invited her to something she couldn't even take her to. She was a terrible person.

"I think it's wonderful that you invited Pilar," Mom said. "I've heard that her family is going through some tough financial times. Her dad lost his job a few months ago and has picked up some night shifts to make ends meet. Let's try to work this out."

"I could drive myself, and you or Dad could take Summer and Pilar," Lisa suggested.

"No, taking two cars is silly," Dad said. "Mom or I will drive you and we'll pick up Pilar."

"Why do I have to go with you?" Lisa complained. "I have my license."

"It's called conserving gas, sweetheart," Dad said. "Don't worry. I'll drop you off a block away so you won't be seen with me."

"I won't. I'll drive you right up to the door and make you kiss me on my cheek before you get out," Mom said. Mom and Dad both laughed.

"Ugh," Lisa said, rolling her eyes. Summer was starting to feel hopeful again, although knowing that Lisa didn't like the plan put a damper on things.

"Lisa, this is a good thing that Summer did," Mom said when she stopped laughing. "We need to support her in this, and since you could get a ticket for driving around a kid who isn't your sibling, this is how we're going to do it."

"I guess," Lisa muttered, looking out the window. Summer tried to think of something to say to make Lisa feel better.

"Thanks for doing this, Lisa," Summer said.

"Yeah, whatever."

Summer felt a tiny knot begin to form in her stomach. If Lisa was upset at Summer for messing things up, then she would never invite her to the mall again. Summer had hoped they could go after her grounding was over. Now the chances of that seemed slim.

Maybe Summer could talk Pilar out of going to youth group. Then Lisa could drive them again, and she would be happier. Pilar wouldn't know what she was missing since she had never been.

Summer could tell her that there were too many kids and the youth pastor had asked them to stop inviting people. No, there was no way anyone at the church would ever tell someone *not* to come to something. Even Pilar would know that.

Then Summer had a truly bad thought. Maybe she could invite Cammie to come, too. She knew Cammie would make a big deal about how lame it was that Pilar was there. Pilar probably wouldn't want to show up.

Summer shook her head. She *was* a terrible person. First of all, Cammie had never shown any interest in youth group. Her family didn't even go to church. Second, she knew she could never do that to Pilar. Youth group was supposed to be fun and safe for every kid, and she wanted Pilar to feel welcome. She was such a nice person.

Summer sighed and leaned back into her seat. Hopefully, Lisa would just get over it and take Summer to the mall sometime anyway. She would do her best not to get on Lisa's nerves from now on.

Chapter 11

The next day in school, Summer walked into choir to see a huge group of kids in a circle. They were roaring with laughter. Summer cautiously approached the group. She was only mildly surprised to see Cammie in the middle of the circle.

"I like tacos as much as the next kid, but come *on*," Cammie said. A few kids snickered. "Do we have to smell them *every day?* What, does she use salsa for shampoo?"

Summer gaped at Cammie. She looked around and didn't see Pilar.

"Cammie," she hissed. "What are you doing?"

"Oh nothing," Cammie said. "Just trying to air out the room. Pilar must have been in here all morning. It smells like Taco Bell." The group of kids shrieked with laughter. Just then Pilar walked in. The crowd scattered.

"Not funny," Summer said.

"Why? What, are you her *friend* now that you have to see her on the weekends?" Cammie said, incredulous.

"No, no, not at all," Summer said quickly. "It's just too soon after the concert thing. You don't want Pilar saying something to get you in trouble, right?"

"Oh. Right. Teacher's pet *PEE*-lar would be a tattle-tale," Cammie snorted.

"I just think you should lay low." Cammie sighed.

"You're right of course. I'll write down all my jokes and save them for later." Summer smiled at Cammie and heaved a huge sigh of relief when she went to get her music.

#

Her relief was short-lived, however. Summer was dismayed when Cammie pulled out a sheet of paper at lunch. It was filled with jokes about Pilar. She hadn't thought that Cammie would actually write them down.

"Alright, Summer, here's what I came up with," Cammie said proudly. Summer cringed and gave Cammie a small smile.

"What are you talking about?" Maddie asked, unwrapping her sandwich.

"Summer told me to write down all my jokes about Pilar, because I shouldn't say them in choir. You know how Pilar might tattle."

"Oh for sure! Great idea!" Brittany said enthusiastically. "What have you got?"

"Wait, *Summer* told you to write them down," Maddie asked in disbelief.

"No! I just told her to lay low so she wouldn't get in trouble again," Summer said.

"Yeah, and then I said I'd write them down, and you agreed," Cammie said. "Anyway, don't you want to hear them?"

"Yes!" Brittany clapped her hands. "We'll pick out your best ones that you can use later." Cammie smiled and began reciting off her list.

"Pilar's mom must drive her to school in a taco cart.

"Have you ever noticed how white her hands are? That's because she spends her free time making flour tortillas.

"I'm surprised that Pilar wears decent clothes. I didn't think her parents got paid that much to clean toilets.

"I totally believe in UFOs. I mean, we have an illegal alien right here in our school...Pilar Sanchez!

"I know why Pilar was so scared of the closet. It reminded her of the box that her family was crammed into when they shipped themselves across the border!"

Brittany and Cammie both laughed so hard that tears rolled down their cheeks. Even Maddie had cracked a smile or two. But Summer was so horrified that she lost her appetite.

"Cammie! You can't say these jokes," she said.

"Why not? They're hilarious!" Cammie laughed.

"They're... they're... *racist*," Summer hissed.

"Oh, they are not. Racism is when you, like, tell people they can't use the bathroom because of their race. Besides, she *is* Mexican, isn't she? You can't deny it, so these are all just, well, factual," Cammie replied.

"Really? You know for a fact that her family is in this country illegally?" Maddie asked.

"Well, no, but that's why that one is funny. Because it's not true."

"It's just a joke, guys," Brittany said. "Lighten up."

"I think Summer has gone soft," Cammie declared. "What do you guys do in that nursery? Does she give you sopapillas to buy your friendship?" Cammie's eyes narrowed as she leaned close.

"You know, Summer, if you like her that much, you can always go sit with her. There is plenty of room at her table. Obviously you don't think I'm funny. Sounds like you're trying to ditch us to make a new friend." Summer's eyes widened.

"I never said that," Summer said. "I... I... just don't want you to get in trouble again."

"Lay off her, Cammie," Maddie said. "She can sit wherever she wants. And I want her to sit with us."

"You'll always be my friend, Cammie," Summer said. "We've been friends *forever.*"

"Okay, fine," Cammie said. "Just so we know where your loyalties lie. Anyway, I need to go to the bathroom before the bell rings. Anyone want to come?"

"I do!" Brittany jumped up. "I've got a Pilar joke too. You know how she's always wearing short sleeves, even in the winter? It must be because she eats hot tamales for breakfast." She snickered.

"That's not really that funny," Cammie said as they walked away. "But I bet I can work with it."

As soon as they were gone, Summer buried her head in her arms. Cammie was getting out of hand. She had no idea what to do.

"What's wrong?" Maddie asked.

"Please don't tell Cammie, but I really like Pilar," Summer said. "She's actually really nice and she's so great with the kids in nursery. She's just really shy at school. I don't know why Cammie picks on her so much."

"Yeah, me either," Maddie said. "I just figured maybe they had a fight last year or something."

"Nope. We didn't even meet her until this year. It's just... Cammie always needs someone to joke about. Last year it was David Davis. She'd always call him 'Davis Davis' and talked about how his mom was so out of it when he was born that she forgot to come up with an original name for him."

"Yikes."

"David had a really good sense of humor. He just laughed it off. He doesn't go to this school this year. I don't really know what happened to him."

"So this year Cammie picked Pilar to be the butt of her jokes," Maddie said.

"I really like Cammie. We've been friends forever. I'm afraid she won't be my friend if I tell her to stop picking on Pilar."

"Well, I think you should just do what you're doing., "Don't tell her to stop, just keep trying to distract her. And I'll really stop laughing at her jokes. Maybe she'll get bored and move on to someone else."

"Maybe," Summer said. She thought Maddie actually had pretty good advice. She didn't need to tell Cammie to stop picking on Pilar. She just needed to distract her every time she brought it up. That way she could still be friends with Cammie and not make Cammie think she was picking Pilar over her. *And* she could still be friends with Pilar without Cammie knowing about it. Summer's appetite returned and she ate her sandwich quickly before lunch was over. This plan would work. Everyone would be happy.

Chapter 12

The McKidd family sat around the dinner table, eating and discussing their day. Everyone seemed to be in a good mood.

"So then Ella came up with this super fun game where you race up the slide, slide down it, run over to the jungle gym and climb up and over, and then run over to the swings. It was so fun!" Faye was saying. Mom and Dad smiled at her. Summer and Lisa rolled their eyes at each other.

"That's great, honey," Mom said. "Lisa? Anything neat happen at school?"

"Not really. I aced my geometry quiz," Lisa said. Dad reached over and ruffled her hair.

"Nice going, Sport!" Lisa ducked out from under his hand and tried to smooth out her hair. She shot Dad a scowl, but smiled a little as she turned back to her plate.

"Summer? Anything to report?" Dad asked.

"Not really," she said. "Oh, Cammie said the funniest thing! She said that Pilar's mom must drive her to school in a taco cart." She laughed. Mom and Dad didn't.

"Summer, that's not funny," Mom said. "That's racist."

"What? No it isn't," Summer replied. "Cammie says racism is when you don't let someone use the bathroom because of their race. This was just a joke. And it's funny, because can't you just picture someone riding to school in a taco cart?"

"Would Pilar have laughed?" Dad asked.

Summer looked around the table, crestfallen. She thought everyone would appreciate a funny joke. Mom and Dad were looking at her with their disappointed faces, Faye was staring at her, and Lisa was quietly eating her dinner, trying to stay out of it.

"Well, no," Summer said.

"Then it wasn't a funny joke. Jokes are only funny if *everyone* laughs. If someone doesn't laugh, then it is probably offensive to them," Dad said.

"And, honey, it *was* racist," Mom said. "Racism is putting unflattering labels on people simply because of their race."

"Well, I *tried* to tell Cammie to stop," Summer said. "But then she said why it was funny, so I thought she was right."

"I know you've known Cammie for years, but it might be time to reevaluate that friendship," Mom said. "I'm not sure I like how Cammie is turning out."

"But Cammie is my friend! I can't just not be friends with her anymore!"

"Well, she seems to be making poor choices lately. Just be careful."

"I will," Summer promised. She was grateful when the topic moved on to something that had happened at work with Dad that day. She was really surprised at how her family had taken the story about Cammie. It made Summer feel a little good to know she had been right to be upset about what Cammie had been saying, but now she was back to square one. She didn't know how she was going to deal with it all.

#

Later, after the dinner dishes had been done and everyone had wandered off to their own pursuits, Summer found Lisa paging through a magazine in her bedroom.

"Hey, Lisa," Summer said, sitting on the edge of Lisa's bed.

"What?" Lisa asked, not even looking up from her magazine.

"Um, I need your advice."

"Word."

"Well, I want to know what to do about Cammie. Can you believe Mom said that I shouldn't be friends with her anymore?"

"Well, it sounds like she's being a dork. Do you want to be friends with a dork?"

"She is not!" Summer cried.

"Saying mean things about someone is dorky. It's totally unnecessary." Lisa finally looked up from her magazine.

"Summer, listen. Pilar probably can hear every word she says. Face it, Cammie is not a quiet person. Pilar knows that you and Cammie are friends. Pretty soon, she's going to think that you are saying the same things as Cammie."

"No way," Summer said. "We're friends in nursery. Pilar knows I'm a nice person."

"A nice person who hangs out with a mean person," Lisa replied. "If there's one thing I've noticed in high school it's that kids hang out with kids who are just like them. You know, the jocks, the band, the science guys."

"Well, we're choir people," Summer said. "That's why we hang out together."

"There are groups within groups. There are nice choir people and mean choir people. It sounds like you are in with the mean choir people."

"Maddie isn't mean."

"Mean always overshadows nice. Look, you have three options. Hang out with Cammie, ignore Pilar, and be labeled as mean. Ditch Cammie and hang out with Pilar. Or tell Cammie to shut up and try to be friends with them both."

"I don't want people to think I'm mean," Summer said quietly.

"Then it's time to make a stand. Don't you remember the memory verse from youth group last month? I know the junior high learns the same one as high school. It was 'Bad company corrupts good morals.' Well, this kind of thing is exactly what that verse was talking about." Summer shifted uncomfortably.

"Okay, thanks, Lisa," she said as she got off the bed.

"No problem," Lisa said, going back to her magazine. Summer walked slowly back to her room, relieved to see that Faye was downstairs watching TV with Mom and Dad. She closed the door to their room. She needed to think.

She wasn't sure Lisa understood her problem. She couldn't just ditch Cammie, even though she knew Cammie was being wrong. Every time she tried to confront Cammie about it, Cammie got mad and acted like Summer didn't like her anymore. But Pilar was so nice and it wasn't fair that all the other kids were laughing at her all the time.

If she decided to be friends with Pilar instead of Cammie, then everyone would probably start making fun of her, too. She did *not* want that. She wasn't the most popular kid in school, but she did like the fact that most people seemed to think she was okay. If she started hanging out with Pilar, Cammie and the whole group would probably make a big deal about it.

The real question was could she stand up to Cammie? Cammie used to be nice. Somehow she had gotten off track. It was probably because she got so many laughs when she was making fun of other people. Summer wished that things could be like they used to. They used to spend their weekends at each other's houses, playing dolls and baking cookies.

Summer decided that Maddie was probably right. She should just keep trying to distract Cammie whenever she started to make fun of Pilar. It would probably be a lot of work, but Summer could do it for the sake of her friendship with both Cammie and Pilar.

Chapter 13

The next day, Summer got to choir before all her friends. Pilar was in there, as usual, studying her music.

"Hi, Pilar," Summer said, smiling.

"Hey, Summer," Pilar replied. She looked up and smiled, but her smile quickly faded. She slumped down in her chair and returned her attention to her music. Summer looked over her shoulder to see that Cammie and Brittany had walked into the room.

"Hey, Pilar," Cammie said. Pilar glanced in her direction, but looked quickly back at her music. "Last night my family went to Casa Bonita for dinner. I'm surprised I didn't see you there. It looked like a Sanchez family reunion was going on in the kitchen." Cammie and Brittany burst out laughing.

"I love Casa Bonita," Brittany said. "Why don't you hook us up with some tacos, Pilar?"

"Seriously. Share the love!" Cammie cried. Several other students began to laugh.

"Hey, Cammie," Summer said quickly. "Can you help me with this music? I'm not sure I'm pronouncing the Latin right."

"Why don't you ask our resident *Latina*?" Cammie snickered. "It's her native language."

"No, that's Spanish!" Brittany said.

"Oh yeah. Sure, Summer," Cammie said. She sat down and looked at the music Summer was holding. Summer glanced over at Pilar. She didn't need help with the Latin. It was just the first thing she could think of to get Cammie to stop talking about Pilar. Distracting Cammie was going to be harder than she thought.

Mr. Camp walked in the room and asked everyone to be seated. He began handing out new music.

"Here's the rest of our music for the Christmas program, folks," he said. "As you know, I'm pretty passionate about music, and I love to encourage all of you in every kind of musical pursuit you choose. In light of that, I'm letting our own Pilar Sanchez accompany us on one piece. I'm not sure if any of you have ever heard her play piano, but she's quite good." He smiled at Pilar. Pilar blushed and continued to look down as she passed the music down her row.

"What?" hissed Cammie. "A solo *and* she gets to play piano on a song? Ugh. It *figures*." Summer patted Cammie on the leg, trying to calm her down.

"I might have to have a talk with Mrs. Dobson about the favoritism being shown in this class," Cammie pouted. "It's not fair."

"Well, if *you* could play the piano, I'm sure Mr. Camp would let you play a piece, too," Summer whispered.

"That is *so* not the point, Summer. What about letting everyone have their shot? Pilar gets *two* at the Christmas concert!"

"You sang the solo at the fall concert, remember?" Summer said. Cammie scowled at her. "And you did really really well," she finished quickly.

"Clearly Mr. Camp didn't even notice because it wasn't his precious *PEE*-lar."

"No way. He couldn't have ignored that standing ovation you got."

"Oh yeah. I almost forgot about that." Cammie's face brightened. She sat forward in her seat and began listening intently to Mr. Camp.

Summer, however, barely heard a word Mr. Camp was saying. Was she really going to have to suck up to Cammie every time she started to make fun of Pilar? Cammie *loved* to have her ego stroked. Summer was worried that they'd never be able to talk about anything fun again, like cute shoes at the mall or the latest Theo James movie. All they ever seemed to talk about anymore was either Pilar or how great Cammie was.

#

Summer and Maddie arrived at their lunch table to see Cammie and Brittany bent over a piece of paper, talking in hushed tones. Cammie and Brittany *never* talked quietly. Summer was instantly on alert.

"Hey, guys," Maddie said. "What are you doing?"

"We're writing a petition," Brittany said.

"Yeah, against Pilar," Cammie said. "We're going to pass it around to the whole choir. It says that it isn't fair that Pilar gets featured twice at the concert. She should only be allowed one thing: the solo or the accompaniment."

"Why?" Maddie asked. "Do you even remember that she was supposed to sing the solo at the Fall Concert, but couldn't because of what *we* did?"

"That was an accident!" Brittany piped in.

"Who cares? If it wasn't for us, she would have had the solo then, and the piano piece now. It is not her fault."

"Whose side are you on?" Cammie demanded.

"You know what? I'm on Pilar's side," Maddie replied. "This little feud or whatever you have going on is so stupid, Cammie. Leave me out of it."

"Why don't you just go sit with her then?" Cammie said.

"Why don't *you* go sit with her?" Maddie retorted. "I'm fine right here, thanks." Cammie snorted and stood up.

"Whatever Maddie. Come on, Brittany, let's go get this petition signed." Brittany quickly gathered the remains of her lunch and followed Cammie to the other side of the lunchroom.

"Whoa," Summer said.

"It needed to be said. I don't have time for these elementary school games," Maddie said.

"You're not to going to sign that thing, are you?"

"No. I mean, I don't think so," Summer said.

"What's to think about? It's stupid."

"But Cammie and I have been friends for so long . . ."

"Ugh, Summer. You can get new friends. You got me, remember?"

"But ditching her seems so mean. I'm not sure I could do it."

"Look, I don't think I'm going to hang out with Cammie and Brittany anymore. They're just going to get us in trouble again. Plus, I'd rather talk about other things than Pilar all the time. In fact, I'll probably sit at a new table for lunch tomorrow." Summer's eyes widened as her stomach tightened.

"No, Maddie!" she cried.

"I understand you've been friends with them for a long time. Just know you can always come sit with me. Cammie and Brittany don't have to be your only friends."

Summer looked across the room as Cammie and Brittany approached kids that were in the choir. She could see some of them laughing and reaching for the petition. Cammie was clearly warming up to her element. She became more animated with each signature.

She looked over at Pilar, who sat alone eating her lunch, blissfully unaware. She knew Pilar would be mortified if she found out about the petition. Summer would have felt terrible if the petition was about her.

Then Summer thought about what Lisa had said last night. Everyone knew that Summer was friends with Cammie and Brittany. Would they think that she had something to do with the petition? Summer blushed just thinking about it. Surely if she didn't sign it then everyone would know she had nothing to do with it.

Of course, she had nothing to do with Pilar getting locked in a closet, not really anyway, and she was punished for that simply because of where she was at the time. This whole Pilar thing was turning into a big mess.

Chapter 14

Summer finished her homework in study hall and then sat with her head buried in her arms. This whole friend situation was really ruining her day.

"Psst. Summer," someone whispered. She looked up to see that Wes had slid into the seat next to her. She glanced up at the study hall teacher. He was absorbed in reading some papers. She looked back at Wes and gave him a small smile.

"You look bummed," he said, scooting closer so he could talk quietly.

"Oh, really?" Summer replied, pleased that he had noticed.

"Want to talk?"

"I don't know. I'm sure it's not really that big a deal."

"It must be if you look that bummed. Usually you look happy," he said, his cheeks turning slightly red. Summer couldn't believe that he knew how she *usually* looked!

"Well, I know this sounds silly, but I'm having friend problems."

"Really? With Cammie and Brittany and Maddie? Haven't you guys been friends since, like, you were born?"

"Kind of. Well, we met Maddie this year. Maddie isn't the problem anyway. The problem is that I'm kind of friends with Pilar now, and you know how Cammie and Brittany talk about Pilar," Summer wrinkled her nose.

"Yeah. The whole school knows how they talk about Pilar," Wes said.

"I don't want Cammie to make fun of her anymore, but I don't want to stop being friends with Cammie, either, and Cammie is making it sound like I have to make a choice."

"Wow. Heavy."

"Yeah." Summer buried her head in her arms again.

"Well, how did you and Pilar become friends? I always see you hanging out with the other girls."

"Um, we go to the same church. Pilar and I work in the nursery together," Summer said. It was the first time she had ever mentioned church to Wes, and she wasn't sure how he would react.

"You go to Life Giving Community? I knew Pilar went, but I didn't know you did," Wes said. Summer was shocked.

"How did you know she went there?"

"My family goes there too. Her family sits near mine."

"I've never seen you at youth group," Summer said, still a little shocked.

"That's because we usually have soccer or basketball games on Fridays. Your family must sit on the other side of the auditorium, or I'm sure I would have seen you there."

"Wow. I can't believe you go to my church," Summer said. Wes smiled.

"I knew I liked you for a reason." Summer blushed.

"Anyway," he went on. "Sorry about the friend thing. That stinks. You know you could always ditch all your friends and just sit with me at lunch."

Summer gulped and stared down at her hands. Then the whole school would be talking about them!

"I, uh..." Summer stammered.

"I'm kidding!" Wes laughed softly. "I know you don't want to ditch your friends. Although it would be fun to eat with you sometime."

"Yeah, maybe some time," Summer said.

"Ahem." The study hall teacher gave them the evil eye from the front of the classroom. Wes smiled at Summer, scooted his seat a little further away and opened a book.

#

That night at dinner, Summer just picked at her food.

"What's wrong, Pumpkin?" Dad asked.

"Nothing. I'm just not hungry," Summer replied.

"She's having friend problems," Lisa said.

"Lisa!" Summer cried. Lisa shrugged and continued to eat.

"What? You didn't say not to tell anyone."

"Is this about Cammie?" Mom asked.

"I... I... don't feel like I can talk about it," Summer said. She shot a dirty look at Lisa.

"I'll be your friend, Summer," Faye piped in.

"Thanks," Summer replied, rolling her eyes.

"Me, too," Dad said. "Don't worry. These junior high problems always have a way of working themselves out." With that, Summer exploded.

"Why do you make it sound like junior high problems are dumb? Or just baby problems?" she cried. "This is not dumb!" Her whole family stared at her.

"I'm sorry, sweetie," Dad said softly. "I didn't mean to make you feel bad."

"May I please be excused?"

"Sure," Mom replied. "But if you need to talk, you know where we are."

#

Later, Summer was lying on her bed staring at the ceiling when she heard a knock on her door. Her mom poked her head in.

"Summer? Can I come in?" she asked.

"Sure," Summer replied without looking at her.

"I just wanted to apologize for how I've been talking about Cammie lately," Mom said. Summer was so shocked she sat straight up.

"What?"

"I didn't realize how much this situation with your friends was bothering you. I'm sure it didn't help for me to be talking about Cammie."

Summer sighed. "It's just that you're right about her, Mom."

"Oh?"

"She's always making fun of Pilar. Always. She never gives her a break, and it's never for any reason. I've been trying to distract her, but Cammie thinks that I would rather be friends with Pilar than her. It sounds like she's going to kick me out the group or something."

"I see," Mom said.

"The thing is, Pilar is so nice! She's so great with the kids in nursery, and, of course, she's great in choir, too. Mr. Camp is letting her sing the solo at the Christmas concert, because she missed the one at the Fall concert, *and* he's letting her accompany a piece because she's really good on the piano."

"Let me guess... Cammie isn't too happy about it."

"No," Summer replied miserably. "She's sending around a petition saying that it isn't fair for Mr. Camp to feature Pilar twice."

"Did you sign it?"

"No! I think Cammie is going to ask me to on Monday. Oh, and Maddie won't eat lunch with us anymore, because of how Cammie and Brittany are acting. I don't know what to do!"

Summer flopped face down on her pillow. She was so embarrassed. Mom sat down on the bed and started rubbing Summer's back, just like she did when Summer was little and upset about something.

"Sweetheart, I know this is hard, but you'll figure it out," Mom said. Summer sat up and faced her mom.

"That's it? You're not going to tell me what to do? Like, ground me from Cammie or something?"

"Nope. I know you know how to treat people. If you didn't, this actually wouldn't be so hard. That tells me that you know what to do. You just have to do it."

"No, I don't!" wailed Summer.

"You're a lot smarter than you give yourself credit for," Mom said. "Hang in there, honey. I'm already proud of you." She leaned over and gave Summer a hug before slipping out of the room.

Summer was glad it was the weekend. She was still grounded, so she didn't have to worry about getting calls from Cammie or Brittany. Maybe she could just not think about it for a few days.

In fact, maybe Cammie and Brittany would calm down over the weekend. Surely they were bored of the whole thing by now. All Summer had to do was wait it out. Things would probably be back to normal on Monday.

Summer smiled to herself and went downstairs to find some dessert.

Chapter 15

Summer entered the nursery with a light heart. She was having a great weekend. She was actually enjoying her time with her family. Lisa had let her hang out in her room on Saturday. They'd painted their nails and looked at magazines. Faye had been acting normal, and not annoying at all. And now she was looking forward to her hour with Pilar and the toddlers.

"Hi, Pilar!" Summer called as she walked in the room. Pilar was already there, pulling out all the toy animals and setting them around the room. Summer couldn't wait to see what Pilar had planned.

"Hey," Pilar replied without looking at Summer. Summer turned around and started greeting the kids who were beginning to show up. They ran to her and tackled her legs.

Summer laughed. She guessed that they were used to her by now. One little girl stood staring at Summer with her arms up. Summer leaned down and picked her up. The little girl gave her a big hug.

"I guess they like me now," Summer said to Pilar.

"I guess," Pilar replied, tucking the last snake under a table. "Okay, kids, it's time for a safari! Line up and be quiet. You don't want to scare the animals away." The kids all cheered then jostled for a place in line. Summer quickly walked over to help them get organized with as little fighting as possible. Pilar began to lead the kids around the room, asking them if they spotted any animals hiding anywhere. Summer trailed behind, keeping the peace among the chatty toddlers.

"Isn't she amazing?" Mrs. Thomas asked, watching the group as they found a lion peeking out from under a chair.

"Definitely," Summer agreed.

"Sometimes when I get home, I write down what Pilar did so I'll have games to play with my kids on rainy days," Mrs. Thomas said.

"Wow. Does she know that?" Summer asked.

"Yes. I keep telling her she should write a book." Mrs. Thomas winked at Summer and went to set up story time.

Soon all the kids were gathered around Mrs. Thomas and Mrs. Lyons. Pilar and Summer quietly began to pick up all the animals.

"That safari idea was amazing," Summer said, smiling at Pilar.

"Whatever," Pilar muttered as she tossed an elephant into the toy box. It was then that Summer noticed that Pilar hadn't even looked at her once since she had gotten there.

"Pilar, what's wrong?" Summer said, worried.

"I'm just tired of you being nice to me here and so mean to me at school," Pilar said.

"What? I'm not mean to you at school!"

"Well, your friends are and you don't do anything to stop them," Pilar hissed. "Don't think I don't know about that petition that Cammie is sending around the school. I'm sure you were one of the first to sign it."

"I didn't sign it!" Summer said.

"Whatever. I'm sick of this. Stop being so two-faced. I don't even know if I can believe you when you're nice to me. You're probably just doing it because you don't want Mrs. Thomas telling your mom or something." Summer was shocked.

"I... I... I can't control what Cammie does," Summer said, suddenly feeling very defensive.

"I bet she doesn't even know we're friends, does she?" accused Pilar.

"Well, no," Summer admitted.

"So you think it's cool to let Cammie think that you agree with her. She's *mean* Summer. And guess what: you're mean too because you hang out with her. Everybody thinks so. Maybe it's good no one knows we're friends. I'd rather everyone think I'm a loser than think I'm a mean girl." Pilar stalked over to where the kids were finishing up their snack.

Summer's face flamed with embarrassment. Everyone thought she was mean? No wonder she got suspended after the concert. She was a part of the mean group that does mean things to kids. She was guilty by association.

Summer slowly tossed toys into the toy box. How on earth was she going to fix this? It seemed like it always came back to her friendship with Cammie. It was beginning to look more and more like she was going to have to make a choice about whether she wanted to be friends with Cammie or not. On one hand, she had been friends with Cammie forever, but her friendship with Cammie made everyone else think she was just as mean. On the other, she could decide to not hang out with Cammie anymore and risk being her next target.

#

Summer was silent all through church, the ride home, and lunch. When she was finished eating, she quietly asked to be excused. She once again retreated to her room. It was Faye's turn to wash the dishes, so she'd have the room to herself. She was glad. She needed some solitude.

Her solitude didn't last long. Soon Lisa came barging through the door.

"Hey, thanks for knocking," Summer cried. Lisa closed the door behind her and sat down on Faye's bed.

"Spill it," she ordered.

"Spill what?"

"You look like you did when we had to tell you that Dad accidentally ran over our cat," Lisa said.

"I do not!"

"Yes, you do. You look really sad about something. Mom and Dad are worried. Just tell me."

Summer sighed. "Pilar said that everyone at school thinks I'm just as mean as Cammie. She practically yelled at me for being two-faced. She thinks that it's good that no one knows we're friends, because then she would be labeled a mean girl, too."

"Whoa," Lisa said. "No one at school knows you and Pilar are friends?"

"Maddie does. I'm not keeping it a secret."

"You are if no one else knows. Why wouldn't you tell anyone else?"

"Um, well, I guess I don't really hang out with anyone besides Cammie, Brittany, and Maddie."

"And you haven't told Cammie?"

"It's just that Pilar gets her so fired up! I don't want her to turn her wrath on me or anything," Summer admitted.

"Listen, Summer, no one will ever say anything bad about your loyalty — I'm amazed at how fiercely you are holding on to this friendship with Cammie — But it almost sounds to me like you are only friends with her now because you're afraid of what she'll do to you if you decide to quit hanging out with her." Summer nodded glumly.

"Friendship should *not* be based on fear," Lisa said. "Maddie sounds like a good friend, and from what you've told me about Pilar, she could be a really good friend too. I really don't think you'll be missing anything if you decide to spend less time with Cammie and more time with good people."

"I...I don't know," Summer said.

"Seriously, Summer," Lisa said, standing up. "As soon as you make a decision, things will get better. What's making this so hard is the fact that you're hovering. Make a choice and stick with it. You'll figure it out." Lisa left the room and Summer flopped back on her bed.

The thing was, Summer really *did* know what she had to do. She just didn't know how to go about doing it.

Chapter 16

The rest of Sunday seemed to pass quicker than normal and soon it was Monday morning. Summer wasn't ready to face her friends yet. She slowly walked to the bus stop, still unsure of how she was going to fix things. She ran the rest of the way when she saw that Maddie was already at the stop.

"Maddie!" Summer cried. Maddie waved and bounced up and down.

"Man, I wish you weren't grounded!" Maddie said. "These weekends have been going by so slow."

"This weekend was my last weekend," Summer replied. "I'm free!"

"Finally! Now we can get back to normal. Maybe you should come over and spend the night on Friday."

"Yeah!" Summer said. She was *very* ready for some quality girl time. "You should see this new nail polish Lisa let me try this weekend. Maybe she'll let me bring it."

"Cool! We'll rent the new Jennifer Lawrence movie—"

Cammie marched up, cutting Maddie off. "So, Summer," she said. "Are you going to sign?"

"Hi, Cammie," Maddie said. "How was your weekend? Mine was good, thanks for asking." Cammie glared at Maddie and shoved a clipboard in front of Summer.

"I'm sorry," she said in a frosty tone, "I don't talk to traitors."

"Traitor? How am I a traitor?"

"Any friend who does not stick by her friends on something that is important is a traitor. It's in the dictionary. You won't sign, you're a traitor."

"Hmm. I'm not sure that's what the definition of a traitor is," Maddie said, staring Cammie down.

"Hi guys!" Brittany bounced up to the group. "Did she sign?"

"She was just about to," Cammie said, handing Summer a pen. Summer swallowed and looked down at the sheet of paper. She couldn't believe how many signatures Cammie had gotten!

"Well, uh, I actually think it's okay for Pilar to do two things at the concert," Summer said quietly. Maddie looked surprised and smiled.

"What?" shrieked Cammie.

"It's just I still feel so guilty about what we did to her. It's kind of our fault that she gets to do two things anyway, so I can't sign," Summer said. Cammie huffed and grabbed back her clipboard.

"You always were too soft. Fine. I won't make you sign if you still feel guilty about something that wasn't even our fault." She marched over to another group of kids. Brittany trailed behind her. Summer heaved a huge sigh of relief.

"Why didn't you just tell her she was wrong?" Maddie asked.

"I don't know," Summer replied, feeling miserable. "I'm not as strong as you."

"Whatever, Summer. You totally are. Cammie is not your only friend at school, you know. Aren't you afraid she's going to turn on you someday?"

"Yes," Summer said, miserable. "Is there any way for me to do the right thing and not have Cammie be mad at me?"

"Probably not," Maddie said. "But seriously, Summer, having Cammie mad at you is not going to be the worst thing in the world. You have me. I don't care what she says. I'll help you."

Summer swallowed and nodded. "Okay."

#

The moment of truth came in choir that day. For some reason, neither Mr. Camp nor the accompanist showed up right after the bell rang. Cammie saw this as her golden opportunity.

"Alright, everybody," she announced, standing up. "I'm sure all I need is a few more signatures on this petition to stop the unfair practice of letting Pilar be featured twice at the Christmas concert. I know a few of you in here haven't signed. Raise your hands so you can sign now."

"Cammie!" Maddie exclaimed in disgust. "Pilar is right here you know."

Pilar's face turned bright red and she buried her face in her hands.

"Sometimes you have to stand up for what you believe in, even in front of the people you are against," Cammie declared. Brittany cheered. A few kids nodded.

"Besides," she added, "if we don't make a stand now, all the minorities in this school will be expecting special treatment. Pilar is setting a terrible example."

That was it. Summer had had it.

"Cammie, that's enough!" Summer jumped to her feet. The room became silent as all eyes stared at her. Even Cammie's jaw dropped.

"Are you even listening to yourself? You're mean enough without throwing around racist comments like that. Pilar has done *nothing* to you. If you are mad enough to pick on someone, it should be Mr. Camp. He's the one making the decisions."

"Sit down, Summer," Cammie said, regaining her control. "I already told you that you didn't have to sign."

"Nobody should sign because it's ridiculous," Summer replied.

"Wait, what? Why are you defending her?"

"Because she is nice and funny and talented, and doesn't deserve to be humiliated like this." she said, squirming under Cammie's death stare. Summer looked over at Maddie to see her smiling.

Go on, Maddie mouthed, giving her a thumbs up.

"Well, maybe you should start your own petition then," Cammie said, tossing her hair. "I didn't realize you were such close *friends*. For that matter, I didn't realize that you were a traitor like Maddie."

"Cammie, I don't want us to stop being friends," Summer said softly. "I just think it's time that you give up whatever you're holding against Pilar. It isn't right."

"My dad says it's *always* right to stand up for what you believe in. If that means losing you as a friend, then I'll do it."

"Oh, Cammie," Summer said. "Look, my offer to be your friend will always be there, but I can't stand by you anymore." A tear dripped down Summer's face as she sat back down.

"Next time you take a stand, Cammie, take a stand against the dirty water fountains," Maddie said. "Now *that* is something we can get behind."

All the kids started to laugh as Mr. Camp and the accompanist came in the room.

"Sorry, sorry," Mr. Camp said. He was shuffling his music and wasn't looking at the students. "We got tied up in a meeting with Mrs. Dobson. Let's get started so we don't waste any more time."

"Wait, Mr. Camp," Cammie said. "I have a petition here for you."

"A what?" he said, looking up. "What for?"

Pilar looked up at Mr. Camp, then over at Summer.

"Well, a lot of us feel it is unfair for Pilar to be featured twice in the concert," Cammie said. "We all signed." She handed the petition to Mr. Camp.

"NOT all of us," Maddie piped in.

"Yeah," Summer said. "I didn't sign." Mr. Camp scanned the petition, then turned a stern look on Cammie.

"Cammie, do you remember why Pilar didn't get to sing her solo in the Fall concert?"

"Well, yes, but why does she get *two...*" Cammie began.

"If things had gone according to *my* plan, she'd only get one this time," Mr. Camp said firmly. "But since she was so rudely prevented from singing her solo at the Fall concert, it is only fair that she gets to sing for this concert.

And I happen to have a Christmas piece that will be perfect for her to play the piano on. I will not change my program just because she wasn't able to sing her solo last time. Does that make sense?"

"Yes," Cammie said quietly.

"And, Cammie, maybe you, Mrs. Dobson, and I should have a conversation about your participation in choir. It seems to be a bit much for you, and I wouldn't want to be the one causing you all this stress," Mr. Camp said.

"No, no need sir," Cammie said quickly. She hurried to her seat and sat down without looking at anyone.

"Good. I'm glad that's settled. Everyone stand up so we can begin our warm-ups. I feel like this class is already half wasted. We don't have a lot of time before our Christmas concert."

Summer peeked at Cammie as she stood up. Cammie was staring straight ahead, face flushed and jaw set. Summer was glad that it was all settled, but she still had a rock in her stomach. She may have just lost one of her oldest friends.

Chapter 17

Summer slowly approached her usual lunch table. Cammie and Brittany were already there. Maddie was nowhere to be seen.

"Hey, guys," Summer said quietly, clutching her sack lunch to her chest. Cammie and Brittany continued to eat without looking up.

"Um, can I sit here?" Summer asked a little louder. Cammie stood up.

"This table is too crowded, Brittany," she announced. "Let's find somewhere else to sit."

"No, no," Summer said quickly. "I'll go. But you're welcome to come eat with me anytime." Summer hurried away from the table, feeling lost. She was standing at the edge of the cafeteria wondering where to sit when Maddie suddenly appeared at her side.

"Not sitting with them?" she asked.

"They wouldn't even look at me," Summer said around the lump in her throat. Maddie looped her arm through Summer's.

"Summer, you did the right thing, even before Mr. Camp shut her down. She'll get over it."

"I'm not so sure. I've known her for a long time."

"Come on," Maddie said. "Pilar's table always has seats." She smiled at Summer and marched in that direction. Pilar was already there. She was reading a book while munching on corn chips.

"Hey, Pilar. Can we sit here?" Maddie asked, plopping down in a seat. Pilar looked up, surprised.

"Um, sure," she said, looking from Maddie to Summer. Summer set her lunch bag down without sitting.

"I'll understand if you want me to go somewhere else," Summer said quietly.

"No, no, sit," Pilar said. Summer gave her a small smile and sat next to Maddie. They ate their lunch in silence for a few minutes.

"Um, Summer," Pilar said, clearing her throat. "Thanks for what you said in choir."

"Oh, sure," Summer replied.

"And I'm sorry for what I said at church on Sunday. I'm really embarrassed."

"No, you were right. I'm sorry I waited so long to say that to Cammie. It wasn't fair to you."

"It really is okay," Pilar said. "*I* wasn't being fair by thinking it would be so easy just to ditch a friend like that. And actually, I really admire your loyalty."

"Wow. Thanks Pilar," Summer said. She felt the weight lifting off her chest.

"If you're going to youth group this Friday, I'd really like to go with you."

"Oh, um, this Friday I was going to spend the night at Maddie's..." Summer said.

"I'll go to youth group with you guys," Maddie piped in. "I went once before. It's pretty cool. Then Pilar can come spend the night at my house, too."

"*Really?*" Pilar squeaked. Summer was suddenly filled with undying admiration for Maddie.

"Sure. Summer says you're cool. I believe her."

"Maddie, you should have seen the game Pilar came up with in the nursery on Sunday,"

Summer said. "It was this animal hunt safari. I would never have thought of that!"

Pilar blushed.

"Sounds cool," Maddie said. "You'll have to tell me about it. My mom is making me get a babysitting job next summer and I have no idea what to do with little kids."

"Pilar has *tons* of games," Summer said.

Summer was surprised at how content she felt. She glanced across the cafeteria to Cammie and Brittany's table. The two of them were talking angrily, no doubt reliving choir. Cammie shot an angry glare over to Summer's table, then jumped up and stalked out of the room. Summer felt a little sadness, but it was overpowered by the joy she felt at having Maddie and Pilar as friends. She had done the right thing and still had friends in the end. True, it didn't seem like Cammie would forgive her anytime soon, but Summer was determined to be open to resuming their friendship when Cammie was ready.

Summer crunched on her chips and smiled at Maddie and Pilar. She couldn't wait for Friday.

Coming Soon

More in the Choir Girls series coming in 2017

Alto Secrets
Harmony Blues
Solo Disaster

About the Author

Victoria Kimble is a wife, a mom of three girls, a full-fledged homebody, a so-so housekeeper, a mediocre musician and has dreamed of writing her whole life. She lives at the foot of the Rockies in Littleton, Colorado and will never take that for granted. Her thoughts live at www.victoriakimble.com.

Connect with Victoria
f: @victoriakimbleauthor
t: @victoriakimble

CPSIA information can be obtained
at www.ICGtesting.com
Printed in the USA
LVOW13s1018151017
552515LV00010B/317/P